GREAT · MOMENTS · IN
ARCHITECTURE

For Evan

architectural greetings

3.3.04

GREAT MOMENTS IN ARCHITECTURE

DAVID MACAULAY

HOUGHTON MIFFLIN COMPANY BOSTON

Other Books by David Macaulay

Cathedral
City
Underground
Pyramid
Castle

A portion of this book has appeared in *The Atlantic*.

Copyright © 1978 by David Macaulay

For information about permission to reproduce selections
from this book, write to Permissions, Houghton Mifflin
Company, 2 Park Street, Boston, Massachusetts 02108.

Library of Congress Cataloging in Publication Data
Macaulay, David.
    Great moments in architecture.
    1. Architecture — Caricatures and cartoons.
2. American wit and humor, Pictorial.   I. Title.
NC1429.M15A46   720'.9   77-15490
ISBN 0-395-25500-7
ISBN 0-395-26711-0 PBK.

Printed in the United States of America

HC LBM PA CRW 20 19 18 17 16 15 14 13 12 11 10

PREFACE

The incredible oeuvre upon which you are about to gaze represents the first serious attempt to assemble between two covers the generally misunderstood and frequently misrepresented drawings of the distinguished twentieth-century draftsman and amateur historian David Macaulay. Although the works of this hitherto neglected artist crystallize the formal and intellectual preoccupations of generations of quintessentially disillusioned visionaries, many of the plates have lain untouched for years. Those that surfaced periodically were more often than not the victims of a misguided aestheticism.

It was not until September of 1976, while still in the grip of a burning fever, that Judith York Newman, Curator Emeritus of SPACED Gallery of Architecture in New York City, insisted rather violently that an effort be made to gather and display as definitive a collection of the works as possible. Upon her suggestion and out of deference to her seniority the SPACED staff began months of careful research, weeks of painstaking compilation, hours and hours of meticulous restoration and almost forty minutes of cataloguing.

Now, from that exhibition, emerges an opus of truly monumental value — a volume unified by its singular perspective and *pointe de vanish*. In addition to the stunning formal plates are included several equally significant although less finished drawings produced during the artist's famed *period rapide*. As if that weren't enough, a selection of only recently discovered preliminary studies is appended that proves beyond a doubt the authenticity of the plates, thus placing the blame for the work squarely and unequivocally upon Macaulay's shoulders.

Great Moments in Architecture, unauthorized by both the Metropolitan Museum of Art and the British Museum, casts a new light and with it the inevitable new shadow, on the perennial inquiry into the spiritual and philosophical meanings of a barely comprehensible, yet expressible and often extraordinarily improvisatory pioneering, etc. . . .

Providence, 1977   K. GREENLAND BARRY

In loving memory of
the grand profession.

THE PLATES

PLATE 1

One of countless identical fragments from Egyptian relief
carvings of the 42nd dynasty. Loosely translated it means
"Have a happy inundation."

Plate II

The Secret of the Pyramid Revealed.
(For a closer shave.)

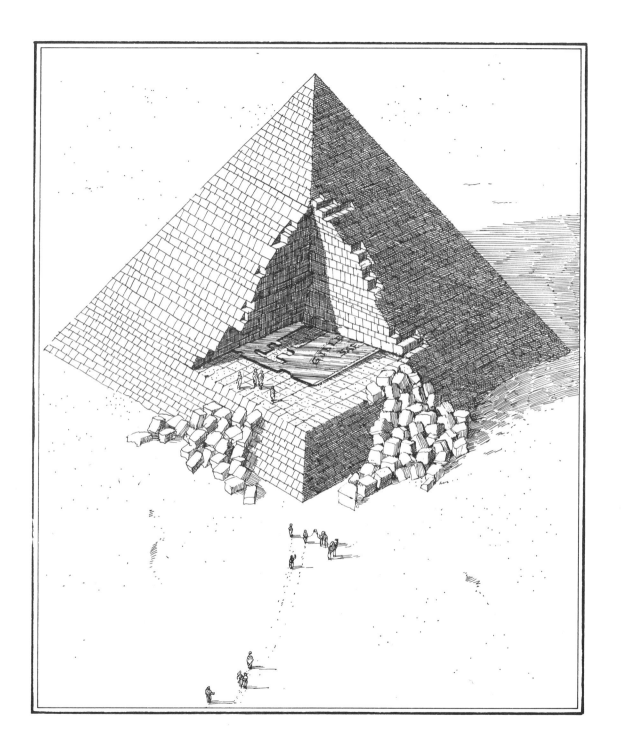

Plate III

Pharaonic Error.
(This plate was formerly titled "Did anyone get that slave's number?")

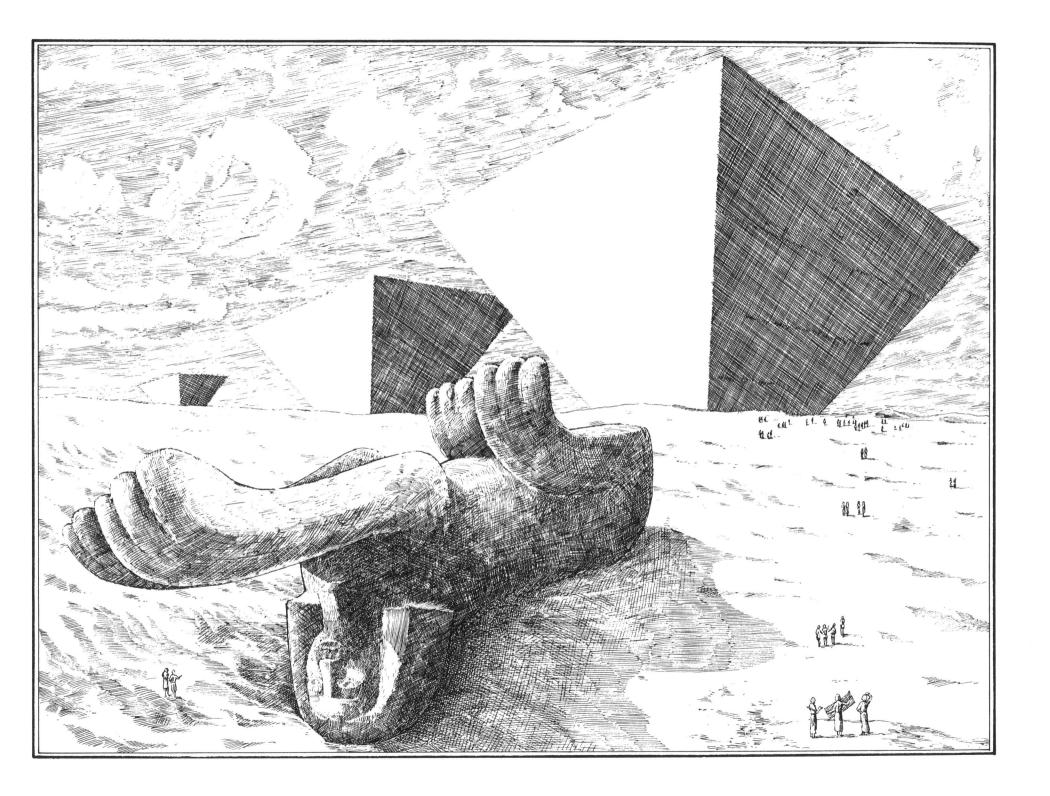

PLATE V

Post Card from Pompeii.
(Owing to a series of strikes at the post office in Naples, this card didn't reach its destination until May of 1913.)

~ Frolicking on the beach at Pompeii ~

This Space For Writing Messages

March, 79

POST CARD

Dear Father,
Pompeii is a nice town.
I met a girl yesterday
near the forum. She
said her father knows
you. Please ask mother
to send my new toga and
the sandals with the little
faces on them. Also money.
Your Son
Pliny

Gaius firstus

Via del Terme

Roma

Special delivery

P.S. Today I lost my job in the vineyard on
Vesuvius. I will miss the wonderful view.

P.P.S. It is getting very, very dark out. I must write a letter to Uncle while
I can still see. Don't forget the sandals, please.

PLATE VI

Late Roman Multipurpose Triumphal Arch.
(Although the bulk of the arch remains buried, Macaulay was reported to have singlehandedly excavated the money basket.)

The Great and Lesser Walls of China.
(This plate was formerly believed to represent the meeting of English and Metric.)

PLATE IX

Leonardo's Favorite Model.
*(From snapshots found in the glove compartment of an abandoned
helicopter.)*

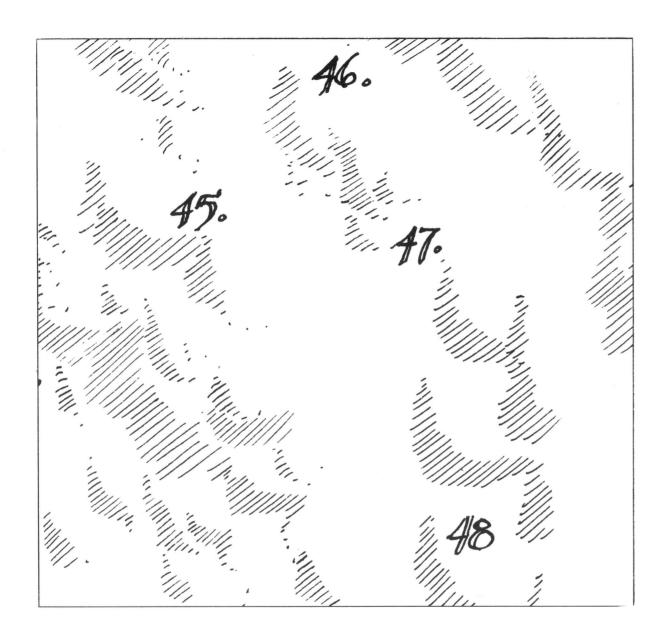

PLATE X

Long dismissed as a simple connect-the-dots game, this plate was finally identified as the "City Churches" of Sir Christopher Wren as seen from 35,000 ft.

Detail of Plate X
This enlargement reveals four of Wren's most famous churches.

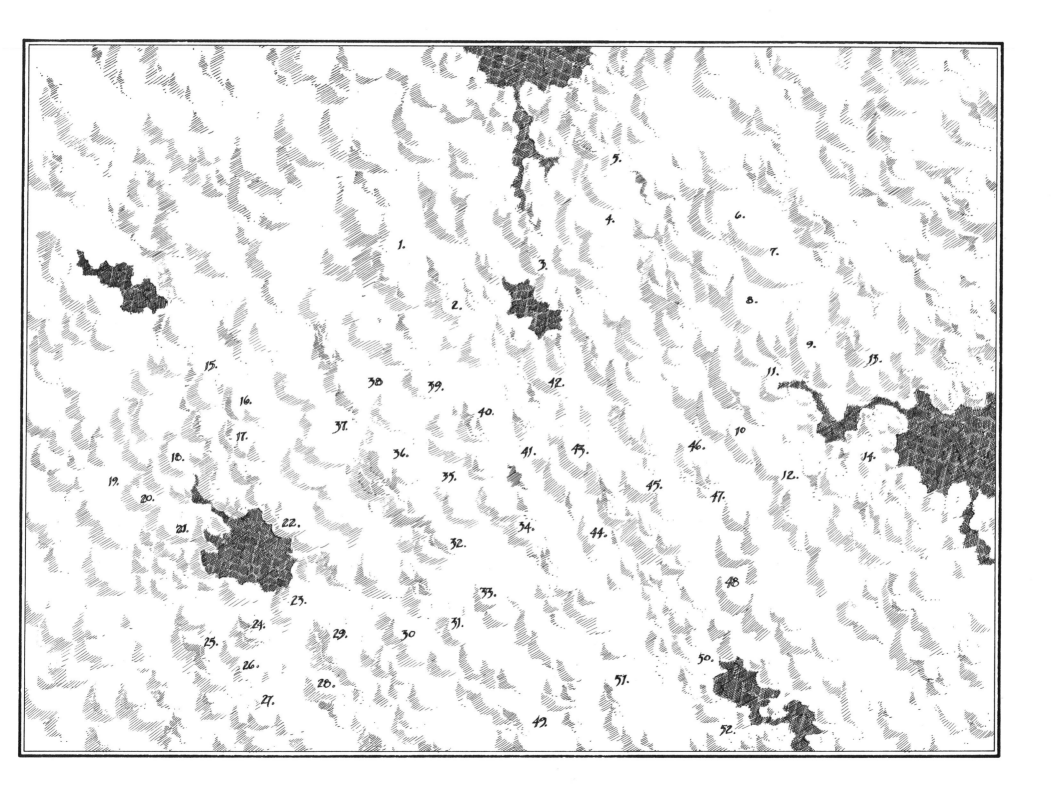

Plate xi

Early Work on the Grand Canyon.

Plate XII

Tour-i-fell.

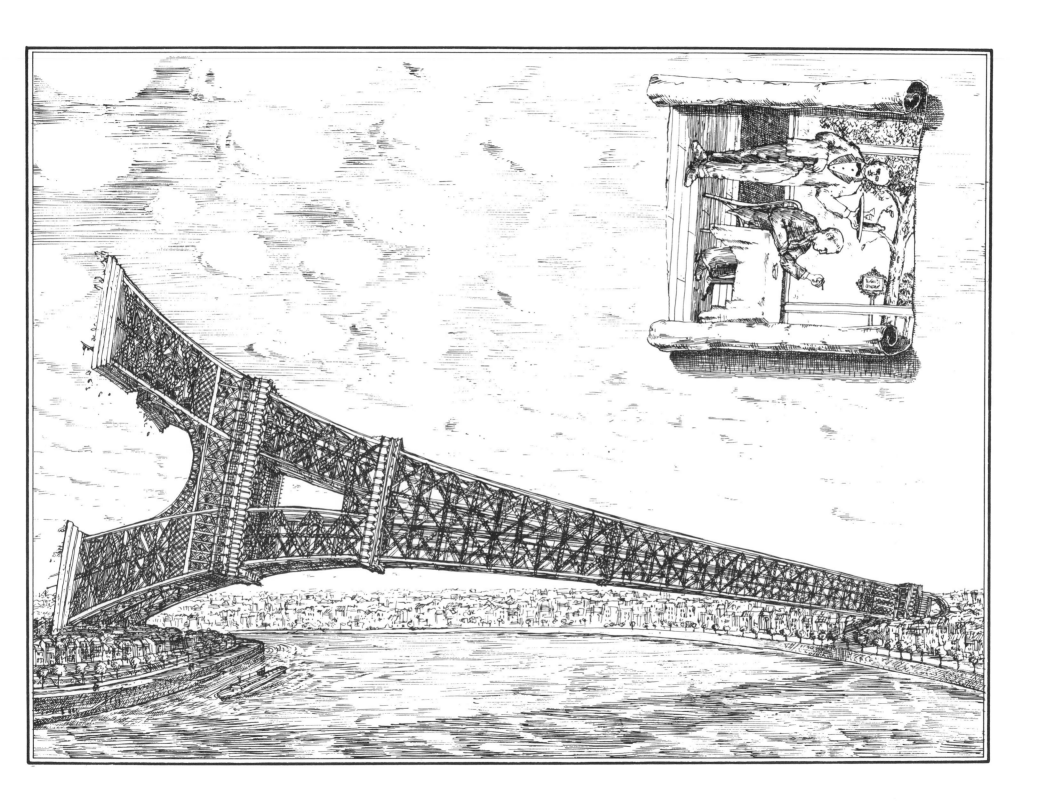

PLATE XIII

L'Arc de Defeat.
(A project designed for Paris, Maine, in 1783 and almost immediately abandoned.)

Plate xiv

Intellectuals Visiting the Tomb of the Unknown Architect.

PLATE XV

Locating the Vanishing Point.
(June 8, 1874)

Plate XVI

Falling Water.

PLATE XVII

Cinder Block.
(From the "Garden of Architectural Delights.")

PLATE XVIII
Door Knob.
(From the "Garden of Architectural
Delights.")

Manhole Monument.
(From the "Garden of Architectural Delights.")

PLATE XX

I-Beam.
(From the "Garden of Architectural Delights.")

PLATE XXI

Fragments from the World of
Architecture.

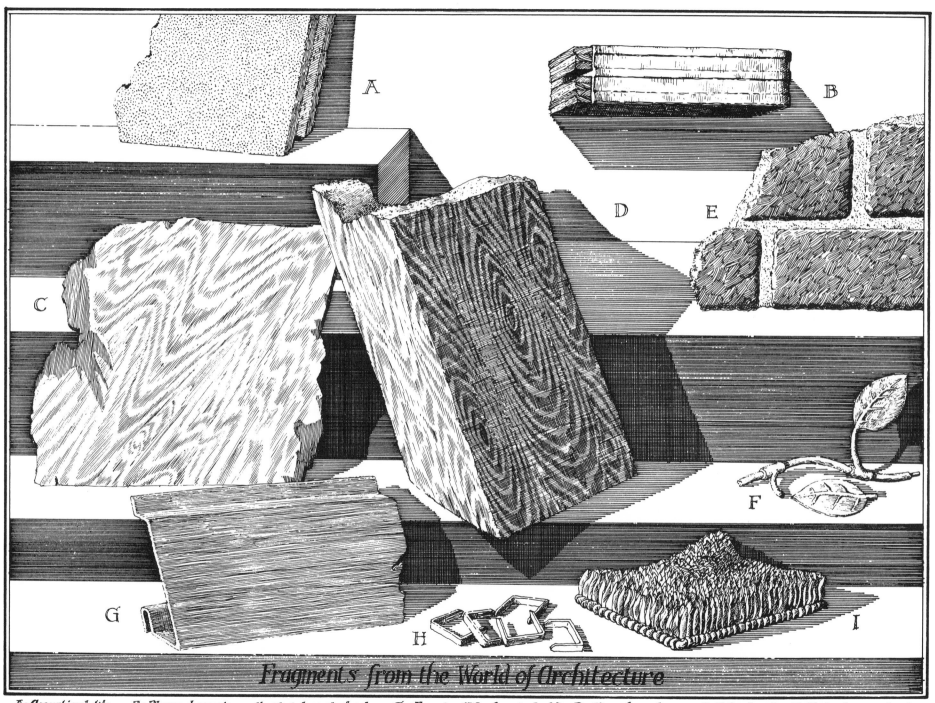

Fragments from the World of Architecture

A- Acoustical tile   B-Plywood counter with stainless steel edge   C - Formica (Woodgrain look)   D-Styrofoam beam   E-Fake brick   F-Fake houseplant
G-Vinyl Clapboard siding   H-Heavy-duty staples   I - Astro-turf

A Tribute to the American Shopping Center.
(For years this plate was mistakenly filed under "Great Moments in Parking.")

PLATE XXIII

Harbor Lights.
(An imaginative example of the successful readaptation of obsolete structures.)

PLATE XXIV

Homage to the Revolving Door.
(After complaining of severe dizziness while gathering the research for this plate, Macaulay was eventually forced to work from photographs.)

PLATE XXV

Homage to the Escalator.
(A rejected proposal for a one-way monument.)

Inflatable Cathedral.
(Yet another abandoned project – this one intended to create a distinguished setting at a moment's notice.)

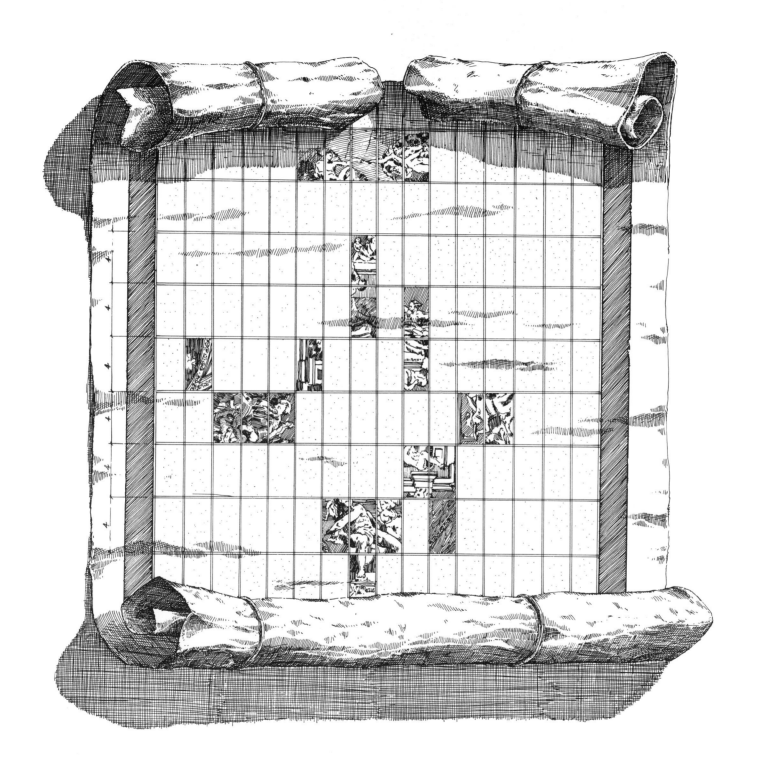

PLATE XXVIII

A Tribute to Vinyl Siding.
(Preserving the Past)

PLATE XXIX

A Tribute to Vinyl Siding.
(Preserving the Future)

A Partially Excavated Fast Food Restaurant.
(In the foreground are plaster casts of the last few customers. Figs. I and II remain unidentified.)

Fig. I

Fig. II

PLATE XXXI

Gas Station.

PLATE XXXII

Drive-In.

Fig. I

Plate xxxiii

Mobile Home.

THE DRAWINGS

VOL. 2, PLATE I

Port-a-Giovanni
(A typical worker's facility from the construction site of St. Peter's.)

VOL. 2, PLATE II

Port-a-Cropolis
(A typical worker's facility from the construction site of the Parthenon.)

The Drawing Board of Giovanni Lorenzo Bernini.

VOL. 2, PLATE IV

The Drawing Board of Tommaso Pisano.

VOL. 2, PLATE V

Noseschwanstein.
(*The project remains unexecuted to this day and so unfortunately does the architect.*)

VOL. 2, PLATE VI

Formal Family.
(The ultimate in topiary accessories.)

VOL. 2, PLATE VII

Oasis.
*(A demonstration of the adaptability of the hung T-bar
ceiling with drop-in 2' x 4' acoustical tiles.)*

VOL. 2, PLATE VIII

An Environmental Consideration.

VOL. 2, PLATE IX

Unfair Warning.

VOL. 2, PLATE X
Planning Ahead.
(Pat. Pend.)

VOL. 2, PLATE XI
Flying Buttress.

VOL. 2, PLATE XII
Too Far.

VOL. 2, PLATE XIII

Small Victory — Highway.

VOL. 2, PLATE XIV

Small Victory — Billboard.

Vol. 2, Plate xv

A Tribute to Vinyl Siding.
(Igloo)

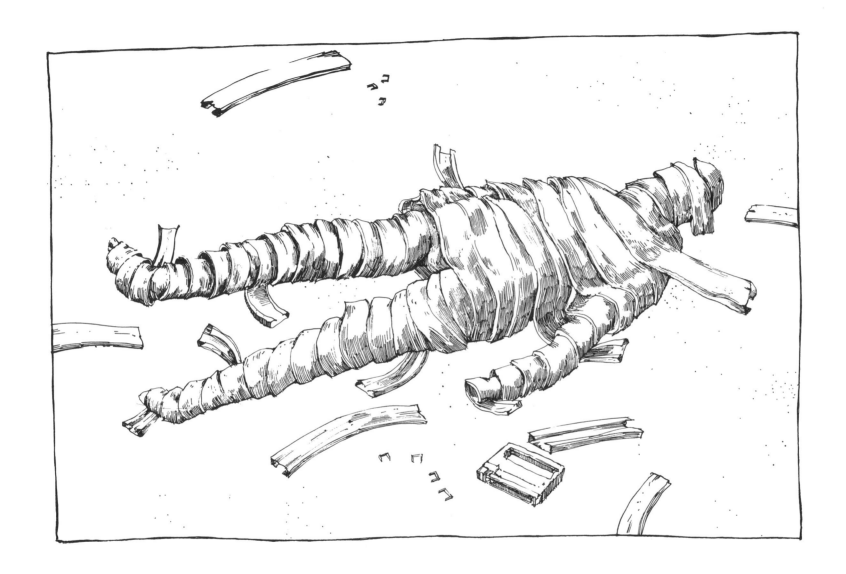

Vol. 2, Plate xvi

Vinylcide.
(An honorable, economical, long-lasting alternative.)

THE STUDIES

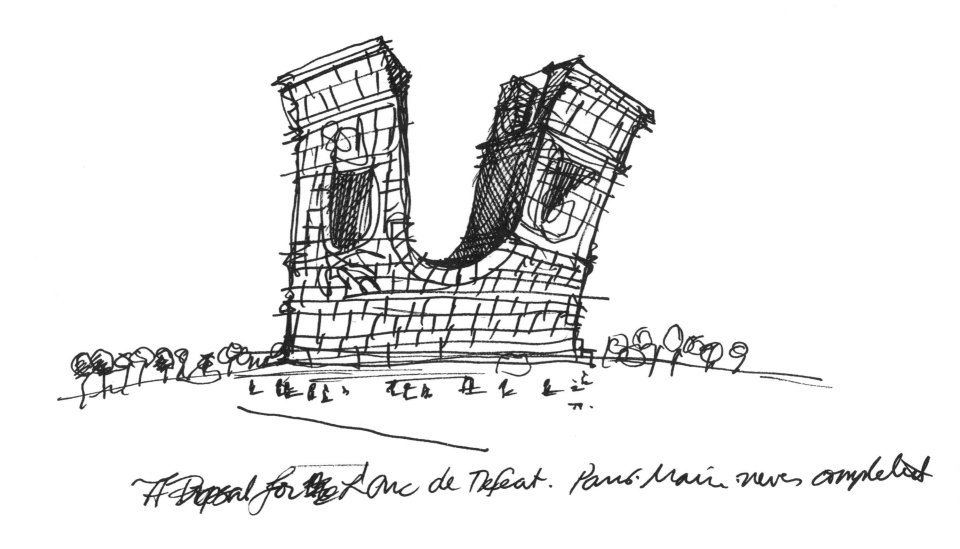

FIG. I

Pencil Sketch for "L'Arc de Defeat." *(actual size)*

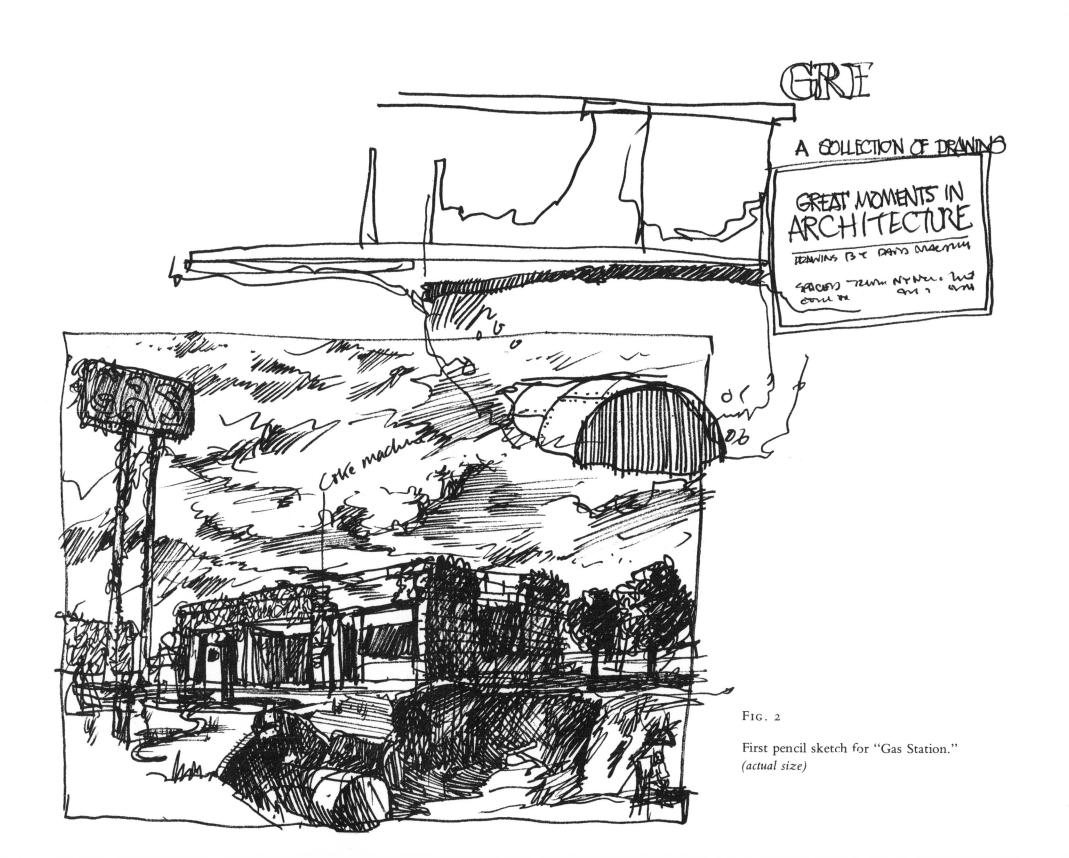

GRE

A COLLECTION OF DRAWINGS

GREAT MOMENTS IN
ARCHITECTURE

DRAWINGS BY DAVID MACAULAY

Coke machine

FIG. 2

First pencil sketch for "Gas Station."
(actual size)

FIG. 3

Preliminary sketch for final preliminary sketch for "Gas Station." *(felt-tip pen)*

FIG. 4

Final preliminary sketch for Plate XXXI, "Gas Station." *(felt-tip pen)*

rubble on ground

FIG. 5

Preliminary sketch for "Tour-i-fell." *(felt-tip pen)*

Fig. 6

Final preliminary sketch for Plate XIII, "Tour-i-
fell." (*felt-tip pen*)

Fig. 7

First sketch from an abandoned project to increase
parking space at the pyramids. (*felt-tip pen*)

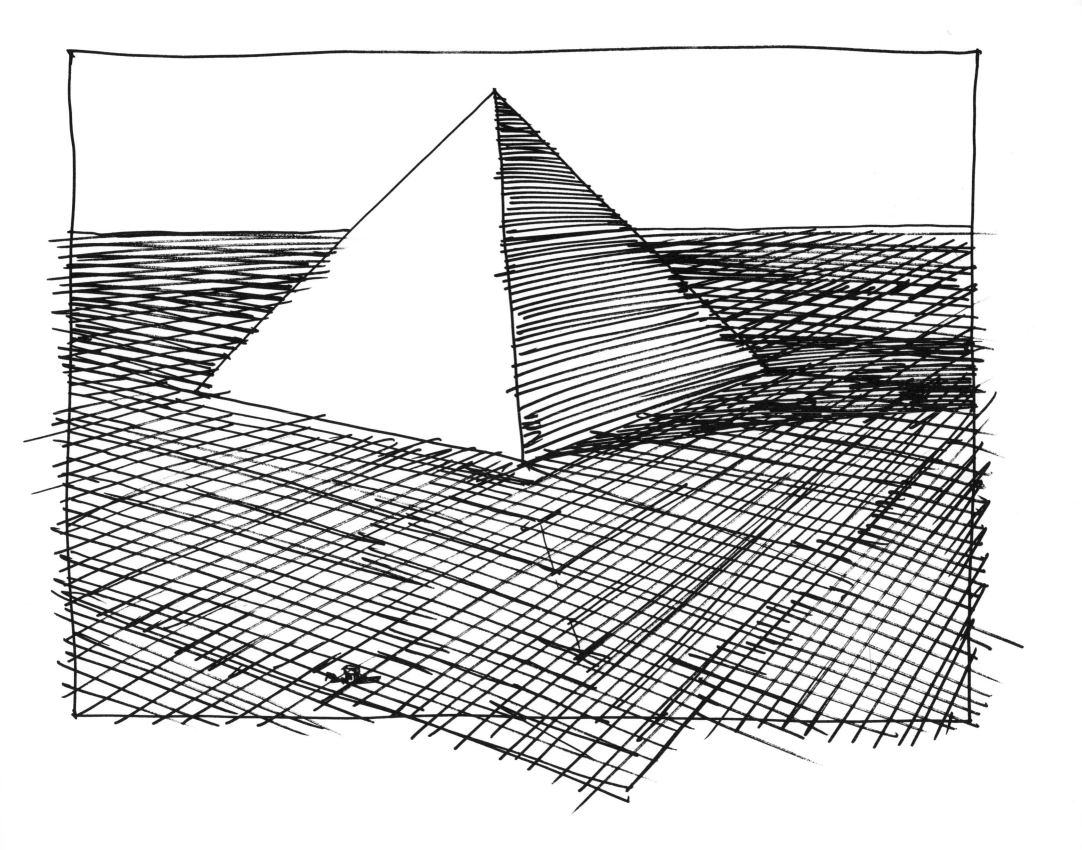

FIG. 8

Preliminary pencil sketch for the final preliminary
sketch for "Homage to the Escalator." (*actual size*)

FIG. 9

Final preliminary sketch for Plate XXV, "Homage
to the Escalator." (*ink and felt-tip marker*)

FIG. 10

Preliminary pencil sketch for the final preliminary
sketch for "A Tribute to the American Shopping
Center." (*actual size*)

FIG. 11

Final preliminary sketch for Plate XXII, "A Tribute to the American Shopping Center." (*pencil and
felt-tip marker*)

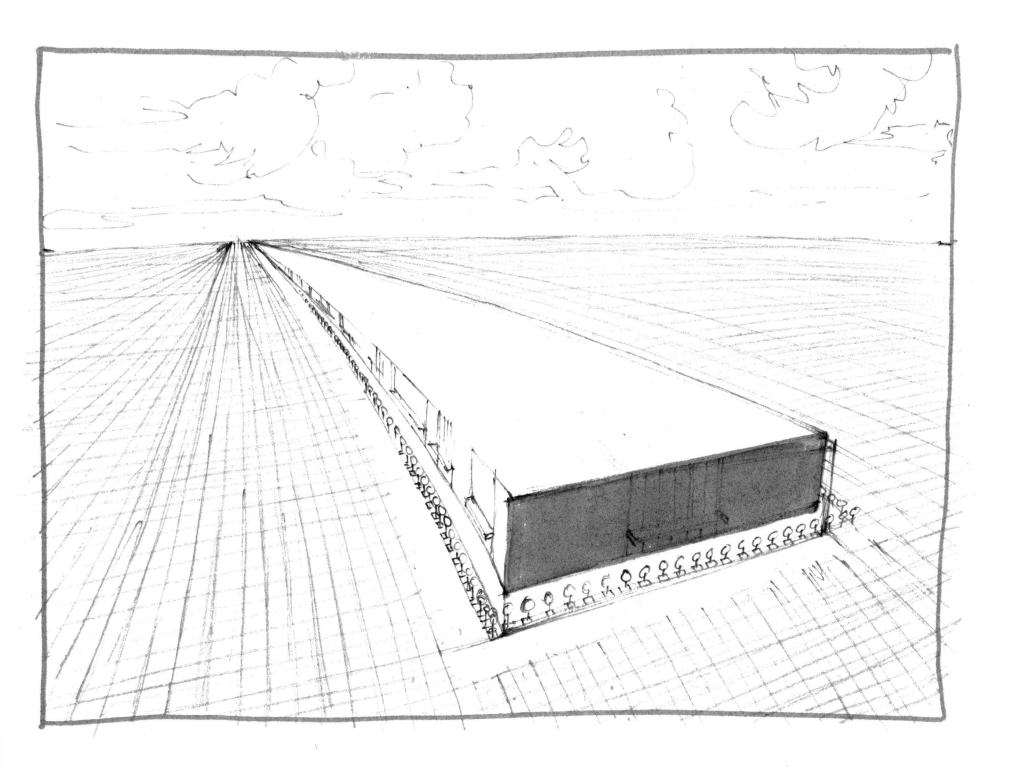

FIG. 12

Preliminary sketch for "Homage to the Revolving Door." (*felt-tip pen*)

FIG. 13

Preliminary sketch for "Inflatable Cathedral."
(*felt-tip pen on balloon*)

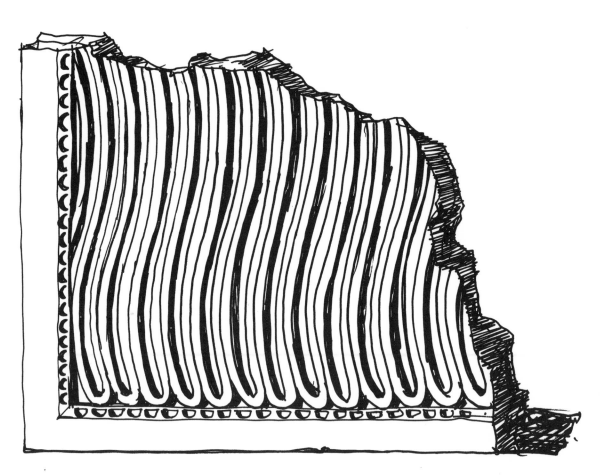

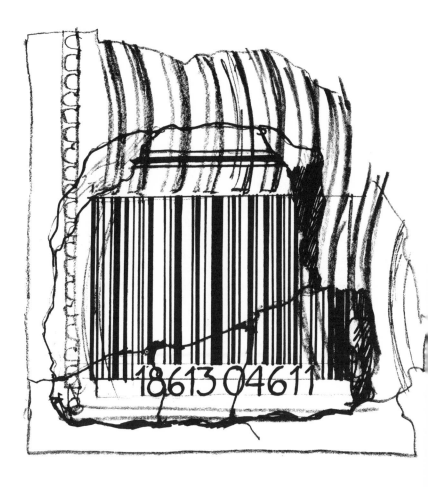

Fig. 14

Study for patterned fragment of Roman sarcophagus. (*felt-tip pen*)

Fig. 15

Study for X-ray of patterned fragment of Roman
sarcophagus. (*felt-tip pen and pencil*)

Fig. 16

Final preliminary sketch for Plate XV, "Locating
the Vanishing Point." (*ink and felt-tip marker*)

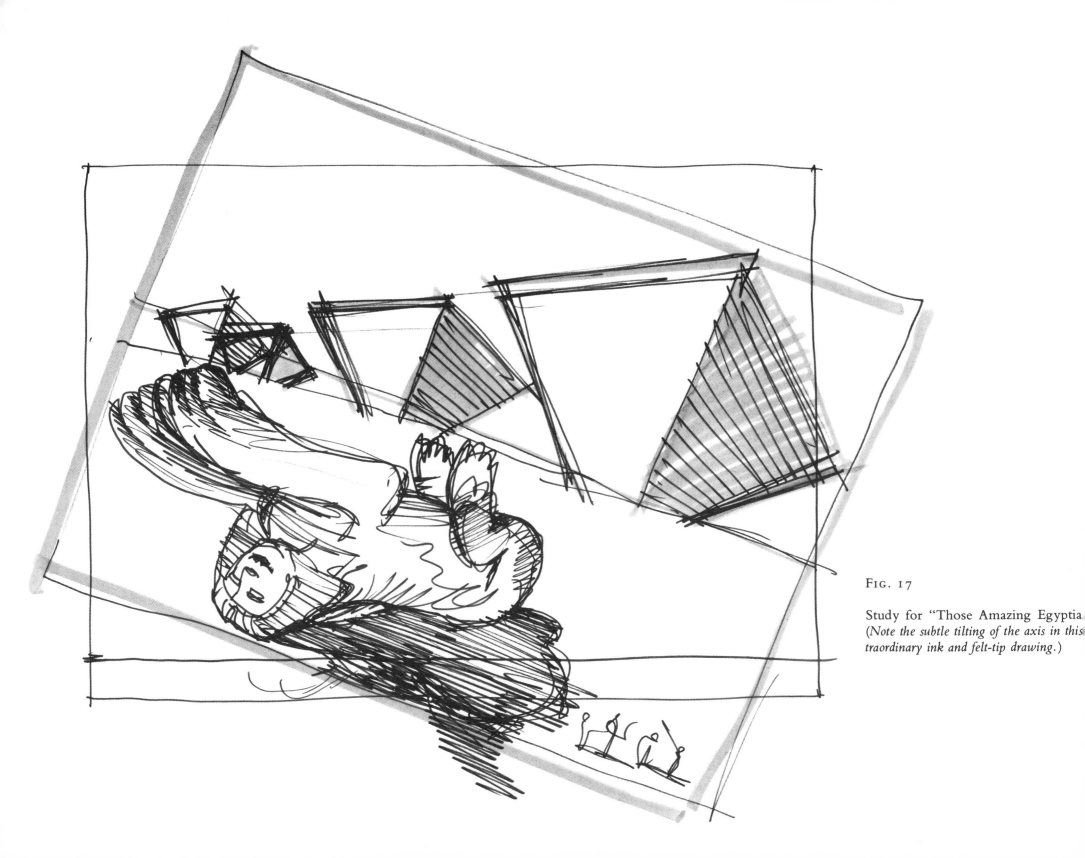

FIG. 17

Study for "Those Amazing Egyptia
(*Note the subtle tilting of the axis in this
traordinary ink and felt-tip drawing.*)

Fig. 18

Studies for "Those Amazing Egyptians."
(*felt-tip pen and marker*)

FIG. 19

Final preliminary sketch for Plate IV,
"Those Amazing Egyptians." (*felt-tip pen
and marker*)

FIG. 20

Study for a hung ceiling in a typical thir-
teenth century cathedral. (*felt-tip pen on
sheepskin*)

FIG. 21

How the Pueblos Used Vinyl Siding. A partial reconstruction of the last partial reconstruction undertaken by the artist before his timely demise. (*ink on sandstone*)

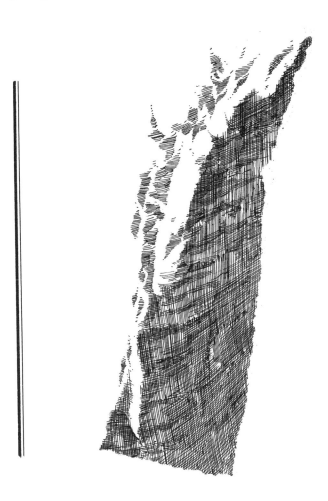

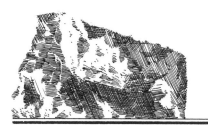